Nathaniel Hawthorne

The Dolliver Romance

Nathaniel Hawthorne

The Dolliver Romance

1st Edition | ISBN: 978-3-75235-710-3

Place of Publication: Frankfurt am Main, Germany

Year of Publication: 2020

Outlook Verlag GmbH, Germany.

THE DOLLIVER ROMANCE

BY

NATHANIEL HAWTHORNE

INTRODUCTORY NOTE.

In "The Dolliver Romance," only three chapters of which the author lived to complete, we get an intimation as to what would have been the ultimate form given to that romance founded on the Elixir of Life, for which "Septimius Felton" was the preliminary study. Having abandoned this study, and apparently forsaken the whole scheme in 1862, Hawthorne was moved to renew his meditation upon it in the following year; and as the plan of the romance had now seemingly developed to his satisfaction, he listened to the publisher's proposal that it should begin its course as a serial story in the "Atlantic Monthly" for January, 1864—the first instance in which he had attempted such a mode of publication.

But the change from England to Massachusetts had been marked by, and had perhaps in part caused, a decline in his health. Illness in his family, the depressing and harrowing effect of the Civil War upon his sensibilities, and anxiety with regard to pecuniary affairs, all combined to make still further inroads upon his vitality; and so early as the autumn of 1862 Mrs. Hawthorne noted in her private diary that her husband was looking "miserably ill." At no time since boyhood had he suffered any serious sickness, and his strong constitution enabled him to rally from this first attack; but the gradual decline continued. After sending forth "Our Old Home," he had little strength for any employment more arduous than reading, or than walking his accustomed path among the pines and sweetfern on the hill behind The Wayside, known to his family as the Mount of Vision. The projected work, therefore, advanced but slowly. He wrote to Mr. Fields:—

"I don't see much probability of my having the first chapter of the Romance ready so soon as you want it. There are two or three chapters ready to be written, but I am not yet robust enough to begin, and I feel as if I should never carry it through."

The presentiment proved to be only too well founded. He had previously written:—

"There is something preternatural in my reluctance to begin. I linger at the threshold, and have a perception of very disagreeable phantasms to be encountered if I enter. I wish God had given me the faculty of writing a sunshiny book."

And again, in November, he says: "I foresee that there is little probability of my getting the first chapter ready by the 15th, although I have a resolute purpose to write it by the end of the month." He did indeed send it by that time, but it began to be apparent in January that he could not go on.

"Seriously," he says, in one letter, "my mind has, for the present, lost its temper and its fine edge, and I have an instinct that I had better keep quiet. Perhaps I shall have a new spirit of vigor if I wait quietly for it; perhaps not." In another: "I hardly know what to say to the public about this abortive Romance, though I know pretty well what the case will be. I shall never finish it.... I cannot finish it unless a great change comes over me; and if I make too great an effort to do so, it will be my death."

Finally, work had to be given over indefinitely. In April he went southward with Mr. Ticknor, the senior partner of his publishing house; but Mr. Ticknor died suddenly in Philadelphia, and Hawthorne returned to The Wayside more feeble than ever. He lingered there a little while. Then, early in May, came the last effort to recover tone, by means of a carriage-journey, with his friend Ex-President Pierce, through the southern part of New Hampshire. A week passed, and all was ended: at the hotel in Plymouth, New Hampshire, where he and his companion had stopped to rest, he died in the night, between the 18th and the 19th of May, 1864. Like Thackeray and Dickens, he was touched by death's "petrific mace" before he had had time to do more than lay the groundwork and begin the main structure of the fiction he had in hand; and, as in the case of Thackeray, the suddenness of his decease has never been clearly accounted for. The precise nature of his malady was not known, since with quiet hopelessness he had refused to take medical advice. His friend Dr. Oliver Wendell Holmes was the only physician who had an opportunity to take even a cursory view of his case, which he did in the course of a brief walk and conversation in Boston before Hawthorne started with Mr. Pierce; but he was unable, with that slight opportunity, to reach any definite conclusion. Dr. Holmes prescribed and had put up for him a remedy to palliate some of the poignant symptoms, and this Hawthorne carried with him; but "I feared," Dr. Holmes writes to the editor, "that there was some internal organic—perhaps malignant—disease; for he looked wasted and as if stricken with a mortal illness."

The manuscript of the unfinished "Dolliver Romance" lay upon his coffin during the funeral services at Concord, but, contrary to the impression sometimes entertained on this point, was not buried with him. It is preserved in the Concord Public Library. The first chapter was published in the "Atlantic" as an isolated portion, soon after his death; and subsequently the second chapter, which he had been unable to revise, appeared in the same periodical. Between this and the third fragment there is a gap, for bridging which no material was found among his papers; but, after hesitating for several years, Mrs. Hawthorne copied and placed in the publishers' hands that final portion, which, with the two parts previously printed, constitutes the whole of what Hawthorne had put into tangible form.

Hawthorne had purposed prefixing a sketch of Thoreau, "because, from a tradition which he told me about this house of mine, I got the idea of a deathless man, which is now taking a shape very different from the original one." This refers to the tradition mentioned in the editor's note to "Septimius Felton," and forms a link in the interesting chain of evidence connecting that romance with the "Dolliver Romance." With the plan respecting Thoreau he combined the idea of writing an autobiographical preface, wherein The Wayside was to be described, after the manner of his Introduction to the "Mosses from an Old Manse"; but, so far as is known, nothing of this was ever actually committed to paper.

Beginning with the idea of producing an English romance, fragments of which remain to us in "The Ancestral Footstep," and the incomplete work known as "Doctor Grimshawe's Secret," he replaced these by another design, of which "Septimius Felton" represents the partial execution. But that elaborate study yielded, in its turn, to "The Dolliver Romance." The last-named work, had the author lived to carry it out, would doubtless have become the vehicle of a profound and pathetic drama, based on the instinctive yearning of man for an immortal existence, the attempted gratification of which would have been set forth in a variety of ways: First, through the selfish old sensualist, Colonel Dabney, who greedily seized the mysterious elixir and took such a draught of it that he perished on the spot; then, through the simple old Grandsir, anxious to live for Pansie's sake; and, perhaps, through Pansie herself, who, coming into the enjoyment of some ennobling love, would wish to defeat death, so that she might always keep the perfection of her mundane happiness,—all these forms of striving to be made the adumbration of a higher one, the shadow-play that should direct our minds to the true immortality beyond this world.

G. P. L.

THE DOLLIVER ROMANCE.

A SCENE FROM THE DOLLIVER ROMANCE.

Dr. Dolliver, a worthy personage of extreme antiquity, was aroused rather prematurely, one summer morning, by the shouts of the child Pansie, in an adjoining chamber, summoning old Martha (who performed the duties of nurse, housekeeper, and kitchen-maid, in the Doctor's establishment) to take up her little ladyship and dress her. The old gentleman woke with more than his customary alacrity, and, after taking a moment to gather his wits about him, pulled aside the faded moreen curtains of his ancient bed, and thrust his head into a beam of sunshine that caused him to wink and withdraw it again. This transitory glimpse of good Dr. Dolliver showed a flannel night-cap, fringed round with stray locks of silvery white hair, and surmounting a meagre and duskily yellow visage, which was crossed and criss-crossed with a record of his long life in wrinkles, faithfully written, no doubt, but with such cramped chirography of Father Time that the purport was illegible. It seemed hardly worth while for the patriarch to get out of bed any more, and bring his forlorn shadow into the summer day that was made for younger folks. The Doctor, however, was by no means of that opinion, being considerably encouraged towards the toil of living twenty-four hours longer by the comparative ease with which he found himself going through the usually painful process of bestirring his rusty joints (stiffened by the very rest and sleep that should have made them pliable) and putting them in a condition to bear his weight upon the floor. Nor was he absolutely disheartened by the idea of those tonsorial, ablutionary, and personally decorative labors which are apt to become so intolerably irksome to an old gentleman, after performing them daily and daily for fifty, sixty, or seventy years, and finding them still as immitigably recurrent as at first. Dr. Dolliver could nowise account for this happy condition of his spirits and physical energies, until he remembered taking an experimental sip of a certain cordial which was long ago prepared by his grandson, and carefully sealed up in a bottle, and had been reposited in a dark closet, among a parcel of effete medicines, ever since that gifted young man's death.

"It may have wrought effect upon me," thought the doctor, shaking his head as he lifted it again from the pillow. "It may be so; for poor Edward oftentimes instilled a strange efficacy into his perilous drugs. But I will rather believe it to be the operation of God's mercy, which may have temporarily invigorated my feeble age for little Pansie's sake."

5

A twinge of his familiar rheumatism, as he put his foot out of bed, taught him that he must not reckon too confidently upon even a day's respite from the intrusive family of aches and infirmities, which, with their proverbial fidelity to attachments once formed, had long been the closest acquaintances that the poor old gentleman had in the world. Nevertheless, he fancied the twinge a little less poignant than those of yesterday; and, moreover, after stinging him pretty smartly, it passed gradually off with a thrill, which, in its latter stages, grew to be almost agreeable. Pain is but pleasure too strongly emphasized. With cautious movements, and only a groan or two, the good Doctor transferred himself from the bed to the floor, where he stood awhile, gazing from one piece of quaint furniture to another (such as stiff-backed Mayflower chairs, an oaken chest-of-drawers carved cunningly with shapes of animals and wreaths of foliage, a table with multitudinous legs, a family record in faded embroidery, a shelf of black-bound books, a dirty heap of gallipots and phials in a dim corner),—gazing at these things, and steadying himself by the bedpost, while his inert brain, still partially benumbed with sleep, came slowly into accordance with the realities about him. The object which most helped to bring Dr. Dolliver completely to his waking perceptions was one that common observers might suppose to have been snatched bodily out of his dreams. The same sunbeam that had dazzled the doctor between the bed-curtains gleamed on the weather-beaten gilding which had once adorned this mysterious symbol, and showed it to be an enormous serpent, twining round a wooden post, and reaching quite from the floor of the chamber to its ceiling.

It was evidently a thing that could boast of considerable antiquity, the dry-rot having eaten out its eyes and gnawed away the tip of its tail; and it must have stood long exposed to the atmosphere, for a kind of gray moss had partially overspread its tarnished gilt surface, and a swallow, or other familiar little bird in some by-gone summer, seemed to have built its nest in the yawning and exaggerated mouth. It looked like a kind of Manichean idol, which might have been elevated on a pedestal for a century or so, enjoying the worship of its votaries in the open air, until the impious sect perished from among men, —all save old Dr. Dolliver, who had set up the monster in his bedchamber for the convenience of private devotion. But we are unpardonable in suggesting such a fantasy to the prejudice of our venerable friend, knowing him to have been as pious and upright a Christian, and with as little of the serpent in his character, as ever came of Puritan lineage. Not to make a further mystery about a very simple matter, this bedimmed and rotten reptile was once the medical emblem or apothecary's sign of the famous Dr. Swinnerton, who practised physic in the earlier days of New England, when a head of Aesculapius or Hippocrates would have vexed the souls of the righteous as savoring of heathendom. The ancient dispenser of drugs had therefore set up an image of the Brazen Serpent, and followed his business for many years with great credit, under this Scriptural device; and Dr. Dolliver, being the apprentice, pupil, and humble friend of the learned Swinnerton's old age, had inherited the symbolic snake, and much other valuable property by his bequest.

While the patriarch was putting on his small-clothes, he took care to stand in the parallelogram of bright sunshine that fell upon the uncarpeted floor. The summer warmth was very genial to his system, and yet made him shiver; his wintry veins rejoiced at it, though the reviving blood tingled through them with a half-painful and only half-pleasurable titillation. For the first few moments after creeping out of bed, he kept his back to the sunny window, and seemed mysteriously shy of glancing thitherward; but, as the June fervor pervaded him more and more thoroughly, he turned bravely about, and looked forth at a burial-ground on the corner of which he dwelt. There lay many an old acquaintance, who had gone to sleep with the flavor of Dr. Dolliver's tinctures and powders upon his tongue; it was the patient's final bitter taste of this world, and perhaps doomed to be a recollected nauseousness in the next. Yesterday, in the chill of his forlorn old age, the Doctor expected soon to stretch out his weary bones among that quiet community, and might scarcely have shrunk from the prospect on his own account, except, indeed, that he dreamily mixed up the infirmities of his present condition with the repose of the approaching one, being haunted by a notion that the damp earth, under the grass and dandelions, must needs be pernicious for his cough and his rheumatism. But, this morning, the cheerful sunbeams, or the mere taste of his grandson's cordial that he had taken at bedtime, or the fitful vigor that often sports irreverently with aged people, had caused an unfrozen drop of youthfulness, somewhere within him, to expand.

"Hem! ahem!" quoth the Doctor, hoping with one effort to clear his throat of the dregs of a ten-years' cough. "Matters are not so far gone with me as I thought. I have known mighty sensible men, when only a little age-stricken or otherwise out of sorts, to die of mere faint-heartedness, a great deal sooner than they need."

He shook his silvery head at his own image in the looking-glass, as if to impress the apothegm on that shadowy representative of himself; and, for his part, he determined to pluck up a spirit and live as long as he possibly could, if it were only for the sake of little Pansie, who stood as close to one extremity of human life as her great-grandfather to the other. This child of three years old occupied all the unfossilized portion of Dr. Dolliver's heart. Every other interest that he formerly had, and the entire confraternity of persons whom he once loved, had long ago departed; and the poor Doctor could not follow them, because the grasp of Pansie's baby-fingers held him back.

So he crammed a great silver watch into his fob, and drew on a patchwork morning-gown of an ancient fashion. Its original material was said to have been the embroidered front of his own wedding-waistcoat and the silken skirt of his wife's bridal attire, which his eldest granddaughter had taken from the carved chest-of-drawers, after poor Bessie, the beloved of his youth, had been half a century in the grave. Throughout many of the intervening years, as the garment got ragged, the spinsters of the old man's family had quilted their duty and affection into it in the shape of patches upon patches, rose-color, crimson, blue, violet, and green, and then (as their hopes faded, and their life kept growing shadier, and their attire took a sombre hue) sober gray and great fragments of funereal black, until the Doctor could revive the memory of most things that had befallen him by looking at his patchwork-gown, as it hung upon a chair. And now it was ragged again, and all the fingers that should have mended it were cold. It had an Eastern fragrance, too, a smell of drugs, strong-scented herbs, and spicy gums, gathered from the many potent infusions that had from time to time been spilt over it; so that, snuffing him afar off, you might have taken Dr. Dolliver for a mummy, and could hardly have been undeceived by his shrunken and torpid aspect, as he crept nearer.

Wrapt in his odorous and many-colored robe, he took staff in hand, and moved pretty vigorously to the head of the staircase. As it was somewhat steep, and but dimly lighted, he began cautiously to descend, putting his left hand on the banister, and poking down his long stick to assist him in making sure of the successive steps; and thus he became a living illustration of the accuracy of Scripture, where it describes the aged as being "afraid of that which is high,"—a truth that is often found to have a sadder purport than its external one. Half-way to the bottom, however, the Doctor heard the impatient and authoritative tones of little Pansie,—Queen Pansie, as she might fairly have been styled, in reference to her position in the household,— calling amain for grandpapa and breakfast. He was startled into such perilous activity by the summons, that his heels slid on the stairs, the slippers were shuffled off his feet, and he saved himself from a tumble only by quickening his pace, and coming down at almost a run.

"Mercy on my poor old bones!" mentally exclaimed the Doctor, fancying himself fractured in fifty places. "Some of them are broken, surely, and, methinks, my heart has leaped out of my mouth! What! all right? Well, well! but Providence is kinder to me than I deserve, prancing down this steep staircase like a kid of three months old!"

He bent stiffly to gather up his slippers and fallen staff; and meanwhile Pansie had heard the tumult of her great-grandfather's descent, and was pounding against the door of the breakfast-room in her haste to come at him. The Doctor opened it, and there she stood, a rather pale and large-eyed little thing, quaint in her aspect, as might well be the case with a motherless child, dwelling in an uncheerful house, with no other playmates than a decrepit old man and a kitten, and no better atmosphere within-doors than the odor of decayed apothecary's stuff, nor gayer neighborhood than that of the adjacent burial-ground, where all her relatives, from her great-grandmother downward, lay calling to her, "Pansie, Pansie, it is bedtime!" even in the prime of the summer morning. For those dead women-folk, especially her mother and the whole row of maiden aunts and grand-aunts, could not but be anxious about the child, knowing that little Pansie would be far safer under a tuft of dandelions than if left alone, as she soon must be, in this difficult and deceitful world.

Yet, in spite of the lack of damask roses in her cheeks, she seemed a healthy child, and certainly showed great capacity of energetic movement in the impulsive capers with which she welcomed her venerable progenitor. She shouted out her satisfaction, moreover (as her custom was, having never had any oversensitive auditors about her to tame down her voice), till even the Doctor's dull ears were full of the clamor.

"Pansie, darling," said Dr. Dolliver, cheerily, patting her brown hair with his tremulous fingers, "thou hast put some of thine own friskiness into poor old grandfather, this fine morning! Dost know, child, that he came near breaking his neck down-stairs at the sound of thy voice? What wouldst thou have done then, little Pansie?"

"Kiss poor grandpapa and make him well!" answered the child, remembering the Doctor's own mode of cure in similar mishaps to herself. "It shall do poor grandpapa good!" she added, putting up her mouth to apply the remedy.

"Ah, little one, thou hast greater faith in thy medicines than ever I had in my drugs," replied the patriarch, with a giggle, surprised and delighted at his own readiness of response. "But the kiss is good for my feeble old heart, Pansie, though it might do little to mend a broken neck; so give grandpapa another dose, and let us to breakfast."

In this merry humor they sat down to the table, great-grandpapa and Pansie side by side, and the kitten, as soon appeared, making a third in the party. First, she showed her mottled head out of Pansie's lap, delicately sipping milk from the child's basin without rebuke: then she took post on the old gentleman's shoulder, purring like a spinning-wheel, trying her claws in the wadding of his dressing-gown, and still more impressively reminding him of her presence by putting out a paw to intercept a warmed-over morsel of

9

yesterday's chicken on its way to the Doctor's mouth. After skilfully achieving this feat, she scrambled down upon the breakfast-table and began to wash her face and hands. Evidently, these companions were all three on intimate terms, as was natural enough, since a great many childish impulses were softly creeping back on the simple-minded old man; insomuch that, if no worldly necessities nor painful infirmity had disturbed him, his remnant of life might have been as cheaply and cheerily enjoyed as the early playtime of the kitten and the child. Old Dr. Dolliver and his great-granddaughter (a ponderous title, which seemed quite to overwhelm the tiny figure of Pansie) had met one another at the two extremities of the life-circle: her sunrise served him for a sunset, illuminating his locks of silver and hers of golden brown with a homogeneous shimmer of twinkling light.

Little Pansie was the one earthly creature that inherited a drop of the Dolliver blood. The Doctor's only child, poor Bessie's offspring, had died the better part of a hundred years before, and his grandchildren, a numerous and dimly remembered brood, had vanished along his weary track in their youth, maturity, or incipient age, till, hardly knowing, how it had all happened, he found himself tottering onward with an infant's small fingers in his nerveless grasp. So mistily did his dead progeny come and go in the patriarch's decayed recollection, that this solitary child represented for him the successive babyhoods of the many that had gone before. The emotions of his early paternity came back to him. She seemed the baby of a past age oftener than she seemed Pansie. A whole family of grand-aunts (one of whom had perished in her cradle, never so mature as Pansie now, another in her virgin bloom, another in autumnal maidenhood, yellow and shrivelled, with vinegar in her blood, and still another, a forlorn widow, whose grief outlasted even its vitality, and grew to be merely a torpid habit, and was saddest then),—all their hitherto forgotten features peeped through the face of the great-grandchild, and their long-inaudible voices sobbed, shouted, or laughed, in her familiar tones. But it often happened to Dr. Dolliver, while frolicking amid this throng of ghosts, where the one reality looked no more vivid than its shadowy sisters,—it often happened that his eyes filled with tears at a sudden perception of what a sad and poverty-stricken old man he was, already remote from his own generation, and bound to stray further onward as the sole playmate and protector of a child!

As Dr. Dolliver, in spite of his advanced epoch of life, is likely to remain a considerable time longer upon our hands, we deem it expedient to give a brief sketch of his position, in order that the story may get onward with the greater freedom when he rises from the breakfast-table. Deeming it a matter of courtesy, we have allowed him the honorary title of Doctor, as did all his towns-people and contemporaries, except, perhaps, one or two formal old physicians, stingy of civil phrases and over-jealous of their own professional dignity. Nevertheless, these crusty graduates were technically right in excluding Dr. Dolliver from their fraternity. He had never received the degree of any medical school, nor (save it might be for the cure of a toothache, or a child's rash, or a whitlow on a seamstress's finger, or some such trifling malady) had he ever been even a practitioner of the awful science with which his popular designation connected him. Our old friend, in short, even at his highest social elevation, claimed to be nothing more than an apothecary, and, in these later and far less prosperous days, scarcely so much. Since the death of his last surviving grandson (Pansie's father, whom he had instructed in all the mysteries of his science, and who, being distinguished by an experimental and inventive tendency, was generally believed to have poisoned himself with an infallible panacea of his own distillation),—since that final bereavement, Dr. Dolliver's once pretty flourishing business had lamentably declined. After a few months of unavailing struggle, he found it expedient to take down the Brazen Serpent from the position to which Dr. Swinnerton had originally elevated it, in front of his shop in the main street, and to retire to his private dwelling, situated in a by-lane and on the edge of a burial-ground.

This house, as well as the Brazen Serpent, some old medical books, and a drawer full of manuscripts, had come to him by the legacy of Dr. Swinnerton. The dreariness of the locality had been of small importance to our friend in his young manhood, when he first led his fair wife over the threshold, and so long as neither of them had any kinship with the human dust that rose into little hillocks, and still kept accumulating beneath their window. But, too soon afterwards, when poor Bessie herself had gone early to rest there, it is probable that an influence from her grave may have prematurely calmed and depressed her widowed husband, taking away much of the energy from what should have been the most active portion of his life. Thus he never grew rich. His thrifty townsmen used to tell him, that, in any other man's hands, Dr. Swinnerton's Brazen Serpent (meaning, I presume, the inherited credit and good-will of that old worthy's trade) would need but ten years' time to transmute its brass into gold. In Dr. Dolliver's keeping, as we have seen, the inauspicious symbol lost the greater part of what superficial gilding it originally had. Matters had not mended with him in more advanced life, after he had deposited a further and further portion of his heart and its affections in each successive one of a long row of kindred graves; and as he stood over the last of them, holding Pansie by the hand and looking down upon the coffin of his grandson, it is no wonder that the old man wept, partly for those gone before, but not so bitterly as for the little one that stayed behind. Why had not God taken her with the rest? And then, so hopeless as he was, so destitute of possibilities of good, his weary frame, his decrepit bones, his dried-up heart, might have crumbled into dust at once, and have been scattered by the next wind over all the heaps of earth that were akin to him.

This intensity of desolation, however, was of too positive a character to be long sustained by a person of Dr. Dolliver's original gentleness and simplicity, and now so completely tamed by age and misfortune. Even before he turned away from the grave, he grew conscious of a slightly cheering and invigorating effect from the tight grasp of the child's warm little hand. Feeble as he was, she seemed to adopt him willingly for her protector. And the Doctor never afterwards shrank from his duty nor quailed beneath it, but bore himself like a man, striving, amid the sloth of age and the breaking-up of intellect, to earn the competency which he had failed to accumulate even in his most vigorous days.

To the extent of securing a present subsistence for Pansie and himself, he was successful. After his son's death, when the Brazen Serpent fell into popular disrepute, a small share of tenacious patronage followed the old man into his retirement. In his prime, he had been allowed to possess more skill than usually fell to the share of a Colonial apothecary, having been regularly apprenticed to Dr. Swinnerton, who, throughout his long practice, was accustomed personally to concoct the medicines which he prescribed and dispensed. It was believed, indeed, that the ancient physician had learned the art at the world-famous drug-manufactory of Apothecary's Hall, in London, and, as some people half-malignly whispered, had perfected himself under masters more subtle than were to be found even there. Unquestionably, in many critical cases he was known to have employed remedies of mysterious composition and dangerous potency, which, in less skilful hands, would have been more likely to kill than cure. He would willingly, it is said, have taught his apprentice the secrets of these prescriptions, but the latter, being of a timid character and delicate conscience, had shrunk from acquaintance with them. It was probably as the result of the same scrupulosity that Dr. Dolliver had always declined to enter the medical profession, in which his old instructor had set him such heroic examples of adventurous dealing with matters of life and death. Nevertheless, the aromatic fragrance, so to speak, of the learned Swinnerton's reputation, had clung to our friend through life; and there were elaborate preparations in the pharmacopoeia of that day, requiring such minute skill and conscientious fidelity in the concocter that the physicians were still glad to confide them to one in whom these qualities were so evident.

Moreover, the grandmothers of the community were kind to him, and mindful of his perfumes, his rose-water, his cosmetics, tooth-powders, pomanders, and pomades, the scented memory of which lingered about their toilet-tables, or came faintly back from the days when they were beautiful. Among this class of customers there was still a demand for certain comfortable little nostrums (delicately sweet and pungent to the taste, cheering to the spirits, and fragrant in the breath), the proper distillation of which was the airiest secret that the mystic Swinnerton had left behind him. And, besides, these old ladies had always liked the manners of Dr. Dolliver, and used to speak of his gentle courtesy behind the counter as having positively been something to admire; though of later years, an unrefined, and almost rustic simplicity, such as belonged to his humble ancestors, appeared to have taken possession of him, as it often does of prettily mannered men in their late decay.

But it resulted from all these favorable circumstances that the Doctor's marble mortar, though worn with long service and considerably damaged by a crack that pervaded it, continued to keep up an occasional intimacy with the pestle; and he still weighed drachms and scruples in his delicate scales, though it seemed impossible, dealing with such minute quantities, that his tremulous fingers should not put in too little or too much, leaving out life with the deficiency, or spilling in death with the surplus. To say the truth, his stanchest friends were beginning to think that Dr. Dolliver's fits of absence (when his mind appeared absolutely to depart from him, while his frail old body worked on mechanically) rendered him not quite trustworthy without a close supervision of his proceedings. It was impossible, however, to convince the aged apothecary of the necessity for such vigilance; and if anything could stir up his gentle temper to wrath, or, as oftener happened, to tears, it was the attempt (which he was marvellously quick to detect) thus to interfere with his long-familiar business.

The public, meanwhile, ceasing to regard Dr. Dolliver in his professional aspect, had begun to take an interest in him as perhaps their oldest fellow-citizen. It was he that remembered the Great Fire and the Great Snow, and that had been a grown-up stripling at the terrible epoch of Witch-Times, and a child just breeched at the breaking out of King Philip's Indian War. He, too, in his school-boy days, had received a benediction from the patriarchal Governor Bradstreet, and thus could boast (somewhat as Bishops do of their unbroken succession from the Apostles) of a transmitted blessing from the whole company of sainted Pilgrims, among whom the venerable magistrate had been an honored companion. Viewing their townsman in this aspect, the people revoked the courteous Doctorate with which they had heretofore decorated him, and now knew him most familiarly as Grandsir Dolliver. His white head, his Puritan band, his threadbare garb (the fashion of which he had ceased to change, half a century ago), his gold-headed staff, that had been Dr. Swinnerton's, his shrunken, frosty figure, and its feeble movement,—all these characteristics had a wholeness and permanence in the public recognition, like the meeting-house steeple or the town-pump. All the younger portion of the inhabitants unconsciously ascribed a sort of aged immortality to Grandsir Dolliver's infirm and reverend presence. They fancied that he had been born old (at least, I remember entertaining some such notions about age-stricken people, when I myself was young), and that he could the better tolerate his aches and incommodities, his dull ears and dim eyes, his remoteness from human intercourse within the crust of indurated years, the cold temperature that kept him always shivering and sad, the heavy burden that invisibly bent down his shoulders,—that all these intolerable things might bring a kind of enjoyment to Grandsir Dolliver, as the lifelong conditions of his peculiar existence.

But, alas! it was a terrible mistake. This weight of years had a perennial novelty for the poor sufferer. He never grew accustomed to it, but, long as he had now borne the fretful torpor of his waning life, and patient as he seemed, he still retained an inward consciousness that these stiffened shoulders, these quailing knees, this cloudiness of sight and brain, this confused forgetfulness of men and affairs, were troublesome accidents that did not really belong to him. He possibly cherished a half-recognized idea that they might pass away. Youth, however eclipsed for a season, is undoubtedly the proper, permanent, and genuine condition of man; and if we look closely into this dreary delusion of growing old, we shall find that it never absolutely succeeds in laying hold of our innermost convictions. A sombre garment, woven of life's unrealities, has muffled us from our true self, but within it smiles the young man whom we knew; the ashes of many perishable things have fallen upon our youthful fire, but beneath them lurk the seeds of inextinguishable flame. So powerful is this instinctive faith, that men of simple modes of character are prone to antedate its consummation. And thus it happened with poor Grandsir Dolliver, who often awoke from an old man's fitful sleep with a sense that his senile predicament was but a dream of the past night; and hobbling hastily across the cold floor to the looking-glass, he would be grievously disappointed at beholding the white hair, the wrinkles and furrows, the ashen visage and bent form, the melancholy mask of Age, in which, as he now remembered, some strange and sad enchantment had involved him for years gone by!

To other eyes than his own, however, the shrivelled old gentleman looked as if there were little hope of his throwing off this too artfully wrought disguise, until, at no distant day, his stooping figure should be straightened out, his hoary locks be smoothed over his brows, and his much-enduring bones be laid safely away, with a green coverlet spread over them, beside his Bessie, who doubtless would recognize her youthful companion in spite of his ugly garniture of decay. He longed to be gazed at by the loving eyes now closed; he shrank from the hard stare of them that loved him not. Walking the streets seldom and reluctantly, he felt a dreary impulse to elude the people's observation, as if with a sense that he had gone irrevocably out of fashion, and broken his connecting links with the net-work of human life; or else it was that nightmare-feeling which we sometimes have in dreams, when we seem to find ourselves wandering through a crowded avenue, with the noonday sun upon us, in some wild extravagance of dress or nudity. He was conscious of estrangement from his towns-people, but did not always know how nor wherefore, nor why he should be thus groping through the twilight mist in solitude. If they spoke loudly to him, with cheery voices, the greeting translated itself faintly and mournfully to his ears; if they shook him by the hand, it was as if a thick, insensible glove absorbed the kindly pressure and the warmth. When little Pansie was the companion of his walk, her childish gayety and freedom did not avail to bring him into closer relationship with men, but seemed to follow him into that region of indefinable remoteness, that dismal Fairy-Land of aged fancy, into which old Grandsir Dolliver had so strangely crept away.

Yet there were moments, as many persons had noticed, when the great-grandpapa would suddenly take stronger hues of life. It was as if his faded figure had been colored over anew, or at least, as he and Pansie moved along the street, as if a sunbeam had fallen across him, instead of the gray gloom of an instant before. His chilled sensibilities had probably been touched and quickened by the warm contiguity of his little companion through the medium of her hand, as it stirred within his own, or some inflection of her voice that set his memory ringing and chiming with forgotten sounds. While that music lasted, the old man was alive and happy. And there were seasons, it might be, happier than even these, when Pansie had been kissed and put to bed, and Grandsir Dolliver sat by his fireside gazing in among the massive coals, and absorbing their glow into those cavernous abysses with which all men communicate. Hence come angels or fiends into our twilight musings, according as we may have peopled them in by-gone years. Over our friend's face, in the rosy flicker of the fire-gleam, stole an expression of repose and perfect trust that made him as beautiful to look at, in his high-backed chair, as the child Pansie on her pillow; and sometimes the spirits that were watching him beheld a calm surprise draw slowly over his features and brighten into joy, yet not so vividly as to break his evening quietude. The gate of heaven had been kindly left ajar, that this forlorn old creature might catch a glimpse within. All the night afterwards, he would be semi-conscious of an intangible bliss diffused through the fitful lapses of an old man's slumber, and would awake, at early dawn, with a faint thrilling of the heart-strings, as if there had been music just now wandering over them.

ANOTHER SCENE FROM THE DOLLIVER ROMANCE

[Footnote: This scene was not revised by the author, but is printed from his first draught.]

We may now suppose Grandsir Dolliver to have finished his breakfast, with a better appetite and sharper perception of the qualities of his food than he has generally felt of late years, whether it were due to old Martha's cookery or to the cordial of the night before. Little Pansie had also made an end of her bread and milk with entire satisfaction, and afterwards nibbled a crust, greatly enjoying its resistance to her little white teeth.

How this child came by the odd name of Pansie, and whether it was really her baptismal name, I have not ascertained. More probably it was one of those pet appellations that grow out of a child's character, or out of some keen thrill of affection in the parents, an unsought-for and unconscious felicity, a kind of revelation, teaching them the true name by which the child's guardian angel would know it,—a name with playfulness and love in it, that we often observe to supersede, in the practice of those who love the child best, the name that they carefully selected, and caused the clergyman to plaster indelibly on the poor little forehead at the font,—the love-name, whereby, if the child lives, the parents know it in their hearts, or by which, if it dies, God seems to have called it away, leaving the sound lingering faintly and sweetly through the house. In Pansie's case, it may have been a certain pensiveness which was sometimes seen under her childish frolic, and so translated itself into French (*pensée*), her mother having been of Acadian kin; or, quite as probably, it alluded merely to the color of her eyes, which, in some lights, were very like the dark petals of a tuft of pansies in the Doctor's garden. It might well be, indeed, on account of the suggested pensiveness; for the child's gayety had no example to sustain it, no sympathy of other children or grown people,—and her melancholy, had it been so dark a feeling, was but the shadow of the house, and of the old man. If brighter sunshine came, she would brighten with it. This morning, surely, as the three companions, Pansie, puss, and Grandsir Dolliver, emerged from the shadow of the house into the small adjoining enclosure, they seemed all frolicsome alike.

The Doctor, however, was intent over something that had reference to his lifelong business of drugs. This little spot was the place where he was wont to cultivate a variety of herbs supposed to be endowed with medicinal virtue. Some of them had been long known in the pharmacopia of the Old World; and others, in the early days of the country, had been adopted by the first settlers from the Indian medicine-men, though with fear and even contrition, because these wild doctors were supposed to draw their pharmaceutic knowledge from no gracious source, the Black Man himself being the principal professor in their medical school. From his own experience, however, Dr. Dolliver had long since doubted, though he was not bold enough quite to come to the conclusion, that Indian shrubs, and the remedies prepared from them, were much less perilous than those so freely used in European practice, and singularly apt to be followed by results quite as propitious. Into such heterodoxy our friend was the more liable to fall, because it had been taught him early in life by his old master, Dr. Swinnerton, who, at those not infrequent times when he indulged a certain unhappy predilection for strong waters, had been accustomed to inveigh in terms of the most cynical contempt and coarsest ridicule against the practice by which he lived, and, as he affirmed, inflicted death on his fellow-men. Our old apothecary, though too loyal to the learned profession with which he was connected fully to believe this bitter judgment, even when pronounced by his revered master, was still so far influenced that his conscience was possibly a little easier when making a preparation from forest herbs and roots than in the concoction of half a score of nauseous poisons into a single elaborate drug, as the fashion of that day was.

But there were shrubs in the garden of which he had never ventured to make a medical use, nor, indeed, did he know their virtue, although from year to year he had tended and fertilized, weeded and pruned them, with something like religious care. They were of the rarest character, and had been planted by the learned and famous Dr. Swinnerton, who, on his death-bed, when he left his dwelling and all his abstruse manuscripts to his favorite pupil, had particularly directed his attention to this row of shrubs. They had been collected by himself from remote countries, and had the poignancy of torrid climes in them; and he told him, that, properly used, they would be worth all the rest of the legacy a hundred-fold. As the apothecary, however, found the manuscripts, in which he conjectured there was a treatise on the subject of these shrubs, mostly illegible, and quite beyond his comprehension in such passages as he succeeded in puzzling out (partly, perhaps, owing to his very imperfect knowledge of Latin, in which language they were written), he had never derived from them any of the promised benefit. And, to say the truth, remembering that Dr. Swinnerton himself never appeared to triturate or decoct or do anything else with the mysterious herbs, our old friend was inclined to imagine the weighty commendation of their virtues to have been the idly solemn utterance of mental aberration at the hour of death. So, with the integrity that belonged to his character, he had nurtured them as tenderly as was possible in the ungenial climate and soil of New England, putting some of them into pots for the winter; but they had rather dwindled than flourished, and he had reaped no harvests from them, nor observed them with any degree of scientific interest.

His grandson, however, while yet a school-boy, had listened to the old man's legend of the miraculous virtues of these plants; and it took so firm a hold of his mind, that the row of outlandish vegetables seemed rooted in it, and certainly flourished there with richer luxuriance than in the soil where they actually grew. The story, acting thus early upon his imagination, may be said to have influenced his brief career in life, and, perchance, brought about its early close. The young man, in the opinion of competent judges, was endowed with remarkable abilities, and according to the rumor of the people had wonderful gifts, which were proved by the cures he had wrought with remedies of his own invention. His talents lay in the direction of scientific analysis and inventive combination of chemical powers. While under the pupilage of his grandfather, his progress had rapidly gone quite beyond his instructor's hope,—leaving him even to tremble at the audacity with which he overturned and invented theories, and to wonder at the depth at which he wrought beneath the superficialness and mock-mystery of the medical science of those days, like a miner sinking his shaft and running a hideous peril of the earth caving in above him. Especially did he devote himself to these plants; and under his care they had thriven beyond all former precedent, bursting into luxuriance of bloom, and most of them bearing beautiful flowers, which, however, in two or three instances, had the sort of natural repulsiveness that the serpent has in its beauty, compelled against its will, as it were, to warn the beholder of an unrevealed danger. The young man had long ago, it must be added, demanded of his grandfather the documents included in the legacy of Professor Swinnerton, and had spent days and nights upon them, growing pale over their mystic lore, which seemed the fruit not merely of the Professor's own labors, but of those of more ancient sages than he; and often a whole volume seemed to be compressed within the limits of a few lines of crabbed manuscript, judging from the time which it cost even the quick-minded student to decipher them.

Meantime these abstruse investigations had not wrought such disastrous effects as might have been feared, in causing Edward Dolliver to neglect the humble trade, the conduct of which his grandfather had now relinquished almost entirely into his hands. On the contrary, with the mere side results of his study, or what may be called the chips and shavings of his real work, he created a prosperity quite beyond anything that his simple-minded predecessor had ever hoped for, even at the most sanguine epoch of his life. The young man's adventurous endowments were miraculously alive, and connecting themselves with his remarkable ability for solid research, and perhaps his conscience being as yet imperfectly developed (as it sometimes lies dormant in the young), he spared not to produce compounds which, if the names were anywise to be trusted, would supersede all other remedies, and speedily render any medicine a needless thing, making the trade of apothecary an untenable one, and the title of Doctor obsolete. Whether there was real efficacy in these nostrums, and whether their author himself had faith in them, is more than can safely be said; but, at all events, the public believed in them, and thronged to the old and dim sign of the Brazen Serpent, which, though hitherto familiar to them and their forefathers, now seemed to shine with auspicious lustre, as if its old Scriptural virtues were renewed. If any faith was to be put in human testimony, many marvellous cures were really performed, the fame of which spread far and wide, and caused demands for these medicines to come in from places far beyond the precincts of the little town. Our old apothecary, now degraded by the overshadowing influence of his grandson's character to a position not much above that of a shop-boy, stood behind the counter with a face sad and distrustful, and yet with an odd kind of fitful excitement in it, as if he would have liked to enjoy this new prosperity, had he dared. Then his venerable figure was to be seen dispensing these questionable compounds by the single bottle and by the dozen, wronging his simple conscience as he dealt out what he feared was trash or worse, shrinking from the reproachful eyes of every ancient physician who might chance to be passing by, but withal examining closely the silver, or the New England coarsely printed bills, which he took in payment, as if apprehensive that the delusive character of the commodity which he sold might be balanced by equal counterfeiting in the money received, or as if his faith in all things were shaken.

Is it not possible that this gifted young man had indeed found out those remedies which Nature has provided and laid away for the cure of every ill?

The disastrous termination of the most brilliant epoch that ever came to the Brazen Serpent must be told in a few words. One night, Edward Dolliver's young wife awoke, and, seeing the gray dawn creeping into the chamber, while her husband, it should seem, was still engaged in his laboratory, arose in her nightdress, and went to the door of the room to put in her gentle remonstrance against such labor. There she found him dead,—sunk down out of his chair upon the hearth, where were some ashes, apparently of burnt manuscripts, which appeared to comprise most of those included in Dr. Swinnerton's legacy, though one or two had fallen near the heap, and lay merely scorched beside it. It seemed as if he had thrown them into the fire, under a sudden impulse, in a great hurry and passion. It may be that he had come to the perception of something fatally false and deceptive in the

19

successes which he had appeared to win, and was too proud and too conscientious to survive it. Doctors were called in, but had no power to revive him. An inquest was held, at which the jury, under the instruction, perhaps, of those same revengeful doctors, expressed the opinion that the poor young man, being given to strange contrivances with poisonous drugs, had died by incautiously tasting them himself. This verdict, and the terrible event itself, at once deprived the medicines of all their popularity; and the poor old apothecary was no longer under any necessity of disturbing his conscience by selling them. They at once lost their repute, and ceased to be in any demand. In the few instances in which they were tried the experiment was followed by no good results; and even those individuals who had fancied themselves cured, and had been loudest in spreading the praises of these beneficent compounds, now, as if for the utter demolition of the poor youth's credit, suffered under a recurrence of the worst symptoms, and, in more than one case, perished miserably: insomuch (for the days of witchcraft were still within the memory of living men and women) it was the general opinion that Satan had been personally concerned in this affliction, and that the Brazen Serpent, so long honored among them, was really the type of his subtle malevolence and perfect iniquity. It was rumored even that all preparations that came from the shop were harmful: that teeth decayed that had been made pearly white by the use of the young chemist's dentifrice; that cheeks were freckled that had been changed to damask roses by his cosmetics; that hair turned gray or fell off that had become black, glossy, and luxuriant from the application of his mixtures; that breath which his drugs had sweetened had now a sulphurous smell. Moreover, all the money heretofore amassed by the sale of them had been exhausted by Edward Dolliver in his lavish expenditure for the processes of his study; and nothing was left for Pansie, except a few valueless and unsalable bottles of medicine, and one or two others, perhaps more recondite than their inventor had seen fit to offer to the public.

Little Pansie's mother lived but a short time after the shock of the terrible catastrophe; and, as we began our story with saying, she was left with no better guardianship or support than might be found in the efforts of a long superannuated man.

Nothing short of the simplicity, integrity, and piety of Grandsir Dolliver's character, known and acknowledged as far back as the oldest inhabitants remembered anything, and inevitably discoverable by the dullest and most prejudiced observers, in all its natural manifestations, could have protected him in still creeping about the streets. So far as he was personally concerned, however, all bitterness and suspicion had speedily passed away; and there remained still the careless and neglectful good-will, and the prescriptive reverence, not altogether reverential, which the world heedlessly awards to the unfortunate individual who outlives his generation.

And now that we have shown the reader sufficiently, or at least to the best of our knowledge, and perhaps at tedious length, what was the present position of Grandsir Dolliver, we may let our story pass onward, though at such a pace as suits the feeble gait of an old man.

The peculiarly brisk sensation of this morning, to which we have more than once alluded, enabled the Doctor to toil pretty vigorously at his medicinal herbs,—his catnip, his vervain, and the like; but he did not turn his attention to the row of mystic plants, with which so much of trouble and sorrow either was, or appeared to be, connected. In truth, his old soul was sick of them, and their very fragrance, which the warm sunshine made strongly perceptible, was odious to his nostrils. But the spicy, homelike scent of his other herbs, the English simples, was grateful to him, and so was the earth-smell, as he turned up the soil about their roots, and eagerly snuffed it in. Little Pansie, on the other hand, perhaps scandalized at great-grandpapa's neglect of the prettiest plants in his garden, resolved to do her small utmost towards balancing his injustice; so with an old shingle, fallen from the roof, which she had appropriated as her agricultural tool, she began to dig about them, pulling up the weeds, as she saw grandpapa doing. The kitten, too, with a look of elfish sagacity, lent her assistance, plying her paws with vast haste and efficiency at the roots of one of the shrubs. This particular one was much smaller than the rest, perhaps because it was a native of the torrid zone, and required greater care than the others to make it flourish; so that, shrivelled, cankered, and scarcely showing a green leaf, both Pansie and the kitten probably mistook it for a weed. After their joint efforts had made a pretty big trench about it, the little girl seized the shrub with both hands, bestriding it with her plump little legs, and giving so vigorous a pull, that, long accustomed to be transplanted annually, it came up by the roots, and little Pansie came down in a sitting posture, making a broad impress on the soft earth. "See, see, Doctor!" cries Pansie, comically enough giving him his title of courtesy,—"look, grandpapa, the big, naughty weed!"

Now the Doctor had at once a peculiar dread and a peculiar value for this identical shrub, both because his grandson's investigations had been applied more ardently to it than to all the rest, and because it was associated in his mind with an ancient and sad recollection. For he had never forgotten that his wife, the early lost, had once taken a fancy to wear its flowers, day after day, through the whole season of their bloom, in her bosom, where they glowed like a gem, and deepened her somewhat pallid beauty with a richness never before seen in it. At least such was the effect which this tropical flower imparted to the beloved form in his memory, and thus it somehow both

21

brightened and wronged her. This had happened not long before her death; and whenever, in the subsequent years, this plant had brought its annual flower, it had proved a kind of talisman to bring up the image of Bessie, radiant with this glow that did not really belong to her naturally passive beauty, quickly interchanging with another image of her form, with the snow of death on cheek and forehead. This reminiscence had remained among the things of which the Doctor was always conscious, but had never breathed a word, through the whole of his long life,—a sprig of sensibility that perhaps helped to keep him tenderer and purer than other men, who entertain no such follies. And the sight of the shrub often brought back the faint, golden gleam of her hair, as if her spirit were in the sunlights of the garden, quivering into view and out of it. And therefore, when he saw what Pansie had done, he sent forth a strange, inarticulate, hoarse, tremulous exclamation, a sort of aged and decrepit cry of mingled emotion. "Naughty Pansie, to pull up grandpapa's flower!" said he, as soon as he could speak. "Poison, Pansie, poison! Fling it away, child!"

And dropping his spade, the old gentleman scrambled towards the little girl as quickly as his rusty joints would let him,—while Pansie, as apprehensive and quick of motion as a fawn, started up with a shriek of mirth and fear to escape him. It so happened that the garden-gate was ajar; and a puff of wind blowing it wide open, she escaped through this fortuitous avenue, followed by great-grandpapa and the kitten.

"Stop, naughty Pansie, stop!" shouted our old friend. "You will tumble into the grave!" The kitten, with the singular sensitiveness that seems to affect it at every kind of excitement, was now on her back.

And, indeed, this portentous warning was better grounded and had a more literal meaning than might be supposed; for the swinging gate communicated with the burial-ground, and almost directly in little Pansie's track there was a newly dug grave, ready to receive its tenant that afternoon. Pansie, however, fled onward with outstretched arms, half in fear, half in fun, plying her round little legs with wonderful promptitude, as if to escape Time or Death, in the person of Grandsir Dolliver, and happily avoiding the ominous pitfall that lies in every person's path, till, hearing a groan from her pursuer, she looked over her shoulder, and saw that poor grandpapa had stumbled over one of the many hillocks. She then suddenly wrinkled up her little visage, and sent forth a full-breathed roar of sympathy and alarm.

"Grandpapa has broken his neck now!" cried little Pansie, amid her sobs.

"Kiss grandpapa, and make it well, then," said the old gentleman, recollecting her remedy, and scrambling up more readily than could be expected. "Well," he murmured to himself, "a hair's-breadth more, and I should have been tumbled into yonder grave. Poor little Pansie! what wouldst thou have done then?"

"Make the grass grow over grandpapa," answered Pansie, laughing up in his face.

"Poh, poh, child, that is not a pretty thing to say," said grandpapa, pettishly and disappointed, as people are apt to be when they try to calculate on the fitful sympathies of childhood. "Come, you must go in to old Martha now."

The poor old gentleman was in the more haste to leave the spot because he found himself standing right in front of his own peculiar row of gravestones, consisting of eight or nine slabs of slate, adorned with carved borders rather rudely cut, and the earliest one, that of his Bessie, bending aslant, because the frost of so many winters had slowly undermined it. Over one grave of the row, that of his gifted grandson, there was no memorial. He felt a strange repugnance, stronger than he had ever felt before, to linger by these graves, and had none of the tender sorrow, mingled with high and tender hopes, that had sometimes made it seem good to him to be there. Such moods, perhaps, often come to the aged, when the hardened earth-crust over their souls shuts them out from spiritual influences.

Taking the child by the hand,—her little effervescence of infantile fun having passed into a downcast humor, though not well knowing as yet what a dusky cloud of disheartening fancies arose from these green hillocks,—he went heavily toward the garden-gate. Close to its threshold, so that one who was issuing forth or entering must needs step upon it or over it, lay a small flat stone, deeply imbedded in the ground, and partly covered with grass, inscribed with the name of "Dr. John Swinnerton, Physician."

"Ay," said the old man, as the well-remembered figure of his ancient instructor seemed to rise before him in his grave-apparel, with beard and gold-headed cane, black velvet doublet and cloak, "here lies a man who, as people have thought, had it in his power to avoid the grave! He had no little grandchild to tease him. He had the choice to die, and chose it."

So the old gentleman led Pansie over the stone, and carefully closed the gate; and, as it happened, he forgot the uprooted shrub, which Pansie, as she ran, had flung away, and which had fallen into the open grave; and when the funeral came that afternoon, the coffin was let down upon it, so that its bright, inauspicious flower never bloomed again.

ANOTHER FRAGMENT OF THE DOLLIVER ROMANCE.

"Be secret!" and he kept his stern eye fixed upon him, as the coach began to move.

"Be secret!" repeated the apothecary. "I know not any secret that he has confided to me thus far, and as for his nonsense (as I will be bold to style it now he is gone) about a medicine of long life, it is a thing I forget in spite of myself, so very empty and trashy it is. I wonder, by the by, that it never came into my head to give the Colonel a dose of the cordial whereof I partook last night. I have no faith that it is a valuable medicine—little or none—and yet there has been an unwonted briskness in me all the morning."

Then a simple joy broke over his face—a flickering sunbeam among his wrinkles—as he heard the laughter of the little girl, who was running rampant with a kitten in the kitchen.

"Pansie! Pansie!" cackled he, "grandpapa has sent away the ugly man now. Come, let us have a frolic in the garden."

And he whispered to himself again, "That is a cordial yonder, and I will take it according to the prescription, knowing all the ingredients." Then, after a moment's thought, he added, "All, save one."

So, as he had declared to himself his intention, that night, when little Pansie had long been asleep, and his small household was in bed, and most of the quiet, old-fashioned townsfolk likewise, this good apothecary went into his laboratory, and took out of a cupboard in the wall a certain ancient-looking bottle, which was cased over with a net-work of what seemed to be woven silver, like the wicker-woven bottles of our days. He had previously provided a goblet of pure water. Before opening the bottle, however, he seemed to hesitate, and pondered and babbled to himself; having long since come to that period of life when the bodily frame, having lost much of its value, is more tenderly cared for than when it was a perfect and inestimable machine.

"I triturated, I infused, I distilled it myself in these very rooms, and know it—know it all—all the ingredients, save one. They are common things enough—comfortable things—some of them a little queer—one or two that folks have a prejudice against—and then there is that one thing that I don't know. It is foolish in me to be dallying with such a mess, which I thought was a piece of quackery, while that strange visitor bade me do it,—and yet, what a strength has come from it! He said it was a rare cordial, and, methinks, it has

24

brightened up my weary life all day, so that Pansie has found me the fitter playmate. And then the dose—it is so absurdly small! I will try it again."

He took the silver stopple from the bottle, and with a practised hand, tremulous as it was with age, so that one would have thought it must have shaken the liquor into a perfect shower of misapplied drops, he dropped—I have heard it said—only one single drop into the goblet of water. It fell into it with a dazzling brightness, like a spark of ruby flame, and subtly diffusing itself through the whole body of water, turned it to a rosy hue of great brilliancy. He held it up between his eyes and the light, and seemed to admire and wonder at it.

"It is very odd," said he, "that such a pure, bright liquor should have come out of a parcel of weeds that mingled their juices here. The thing is a folly,—it is one of those compositions in which the chemists—the cabalists, perhaps—used to combine what they thought the virtues of many plants, thinking that something would result in the whole, which was not in either of them, and a new efficacy be created. Whereas, it has been the teaching of my experience that one virtue counteracts another, and is the enemy of it. I never believed the former theory, even when that strange madman bade me do it. And what a thick, turbid matter it was, until that last ingredient,—that powder which he put in with his own hand! Had he let me see it, I would first have analyzed it, and discovered its component parts. The man was mad, undoubtedly, and this may have been poison. But its effect is good. Poh! I will taste again, because of this weak, agued, miserable state of mine; though it is a shame in me, a man of decent skill in my way, to believe in a quack's nostrum. But it is a comfortable kind of thing."

Meantime, that single drop (for good Dr. Dolliver had immediately put a stopper into the bottle) diffused a sweet odor through the chamber, so that the ordinary fragrances and scents of apothecaries' stuff seemed to be controlled and influenced by it, and its bright potency also dispelled a certain dimness of the antiquated room.

The Doctor, at the pressure of a great need, had given incredible pains to the manufacture of this medicine; so that, reckoning the pains rather than the ingredients (all except one, of which he was not able to estimate the cost nor value), it was really worth its weight in gold. And, as it happened, he had bestowed upon it the hard labor of his poor life, and the time that was necessary for the support of his family, without return; for the customers, after playing off this cruel joke upon the old man, had never come back; and now, for seven years, the bottle had stood in a corner of the cupboard. To be sure, the silver-cased bottle was worth a trifle for its silver, and still more, perhaps, as an antiquarian knick-knack. But, all things considered, the honest and simple apothecary thought that he might make free with the liquid to such small extent as was necessary for himself. And there had been something in the concoction that had struck him; and he had been fast breaking lately; and so, in the dreary fantasy and lonely recklessness of his old age, he had suddenly bethought himself of this medicine (cordial,—as the strange man called it, which had come to him by long inheritance in his family) and he had determined to try it. And again, as the night before, he took out the receipt—a roll of antique parchment, out of which, provokingly, one fold had been lost—and put on his spectacles to puzzle out the passage.

Guttam unicam in aquam puram, two gills. "If the Colonel should hear of this," said Dr. Dolliver, "he might fancy it his nostrum of long life, and insist on having the bottle for his own use. The foolish, fierce old gentleman! He has grown very earthly, of late, else he would not desire such a thing. And a strong desire it must be to make him feel it desirable. For my part, I only wish for something that, for a short time, may clear my eyes, so that I may see little Pansie's beauty, and quicken my ears, that I may hear her sweet voice, and give me nerve, while God keeps me here, that I may live longer to earn bread for dear Pansie. She provided for, I would gladly lie down yonder with Bessie and our children. Ah! the vanity of desiring lengthened days!—There!—I have drunk it, and methinks its final, subtle flavor hath strange potency in it."

The old man shivered a little, as those shiver who have just swallowed good liquor, while it is permeating their vitals. Yet he seemed to be in a pleasant state of feeling, and, as was frequently the case with this simple soul, in a devout frame of mind. He read a chapter in the Bible, and said his prayers for Pansie and himself, before he went to bed, and had much better sleep than usually comes to people of his advanced age; for, at that period, sleep is diffused through their wakefulness, and a dim and tiresome half-perception through their sleep, so that the only result is weariness.

Nothing very extraordinary happened to Dr. Dolliver or his small household for some time afterwards. He was favored with a comfortable winter, and thanked Heaven for it, and put it to a good use (at least he intended it so) by concocting drugs; which perhaps did a little towards peopling the graveyard, into which his windows looked; but that was neither his purpose nor his fault. None of the sleepers, at all events, interrupted their slumbers to upbraid him. He had done according to his own artless conscience and the recipes of licensed physicians, and he looked no further, but pounded, triturated, infused, made electuaries, boluses, juleps, or whatever he termed his productions, with skill and diligence, thanking Heaven that he was spared to do so, when his contemporaries generally were getting incapable of similar efforts. It struck him with some surprise, but much gratitude to Providence, that his sight seemed to be growing rather better than worse. He certainly could read the crabbed handwriting and hieroglyphics of the physicians with more readiness than he could a year earlier. But he had been originally near-sighted, with large, projecting eyes; and near-sighted eyes always seem to get a new lease of light as the years go on. One thing was perceptible about the Doctor's eyes, not only to himself in the glass, but to everybody else; namely, that they had an unaccustomed gleaming brightness in them; not so very bright either, but yet so much so, that little Pansie noticed it, and sometimes, in her playful, roguish way, climbed up into his lap, and put both her small palms over them; telling Grandpapa that he had stolen somebody else's eyes, and given away his own, and that she liked his old ones better. The poor old Doctor did his best to smile through his eyes, and so to reconcile Pansie to their brightness: but still she continually made the same silly remonstrance, so that he was fain to put on a pair of green spectacles when he was going to play with Pansie, or took her on his knee. Nay, if he looked at her, as had always been his custom, after she was asleep, in order to see that all was well with her, the little child would put up her hands, as if he held a light that was flashing on her eyeballs; and unless he turned away his gaze quickly, she would wake up in a fit of crying.

On the whole, the apothecary had as comfortable a time as a man of his years could expect. The air of the house and of the old graveyard seemed to suit him. What so seldom happens in man's advancing age, his night's rest did him good, whereas, generally, an old man wakes up ten times as nervous and dispirited as he went to bed, just as if, during his sleep he had been working harder than ever he did in the daytime. It had been so with the Doctor himself till within a few months. To be sure, he had latterly begun to practise various rules of diet and exercise, which commended themselves to his approbation. He sawed some of his own fire-wood, and fancied that, as was reasonable, it fatigued him less day by day. He took walks with Pansie, and though, of course, her little footsteps, treading on the elastic air of childhood, far outstripped his own, still the old man knew that he was not beyond the recuperative period of life, and that exercise out of doors and proper food can do somewhat towards retarding the approach of age. He was inclined, also, to impute much good effect to a daily dose of Santa Cruz rum (a liquor much in vogue in that day), which he was now in the habit of quaffing at the meridian hour. All through the Doctor's life he had eschewed strong spirits: "But after seventy," quoth old Dr. Dolliver, "a man is all the better in head and stomach for a little stimulus"; and it certainly seemed so in his case. Likewise, I know not precisely how often, but complying punctiliously with the recipe, as an apothecary naturally would, he took his drop of the mysterious cordial.

He was inclined, however, to impute little or no efficacy to this, and to laugh at himself for having ever thought otherwise. The dose was so very minute! and he had never been sensible of any remarkable effect on taking it, after all. A genial warmth, he sometimes fancied, diffused itself throughout him, and perhaps continued during the next day. A quiet and refreshing night's rest followed, and alacritous waking in the morning; but all this was far more probably owing, as has been already hinted, to excellent and well-considered habits of diet and exercise. Nevertheless he still continued the cordial with tolerable regularity,—the more, because on one or two occasions, happening to omit it, it so chanced that he slept wretchedly, and awoke in strange aches and pains, torpors, nervousness, shaking of the hands, bleared-ness of sight, lowness of spirits and other ills, as is the misfortune of some old men,—who are often threatened by a thousand evil symptoms that come to nothing, foreboding no particular disorder, and passing away as unsatisfactorily as they come. At another time, he took two or three drops at once, and was alarmingly feverish in consequence. Yet it was very true, that the feverish symptoms were pretty sure to disappear on his renewal of the medicine. "Still it could not be that," thought the old man, a hater of empiricism (in which, however, is contained all hope for man), and disinclined to believe in anything that was not according to rule and art. And then, as aforesaid, the dose was so ridiculously small!

Sometimes, however, he took, half laughingly, another view of it, and felt disposed to think that chance might really have thrown in his way a very remarkable mixture, by which, if it had happened to him earlier in life, he might have amassed a larger fortune, and might even have raked together such a competency as would have prevented his feeling much uneasiness about the future of little Pansie. Feeling as strong as he did nowadays, he might reasonably count upon ten years more of life, and in that time the precious liquor might be exchanged for much gold. "Let us see!" quoth he, "by what attractive name shall it be advertised? 'The old man's cordial?' That promises too little. Poh, poh! I would stain my honesty, my fair reputation, the accumulation of a lifetime, and befool my neighbor and the public, by any name that would make them imagine I had found that ridiculous talisman that the alchemists have sought. The old man's cordial,—that is best. And five shillings sterling the bottle. That surely were not too costly, and would give the medicine a better reputation and higher vogue (so foolish is the world) than if I were to put it lower. I will think further of this. But pshaw, pshaw!"

"What is the matter. Grandpapa," said little Pansie, who had stood by him, wishing to speak to him at least a minute, but had been deterred by his absorption; "why do you say 'Pshaw'?"

"Pshaw!" repeated Grandpapa, "there is one ingredient that I don't know."

So this very hopeful design was necessarily given up, but that it had occurred to Dr. Dolliver was perhaps a token that his mind was in a very vigorous state; for it had been noted of him through life, that he had little enterprise, little activity, and that, for the want of these things, his very considerable skill in his art had been almost thrown away, as regarded his private affairs, when it might easily have led him to fortune. Whereas, here in his extreme age, he had first bethought himself of a way to grow rich. Sometimes this latter spring causes—as blossoms come on the autumnal tree—a spurt of vigor, or untimely greenness, when Nature laughs at her old child, half in kindness and half in scorn. It is observable, however, I fancy, that after such a spurt, age comes on with redoubled speed, and that the old man has only run forward with a show of force, in order to fall into his grave the sooner.

Sometimes, as he was walking briskly along the street, with little Pansie clasping his hand, and perhaps frisking rather more than became a person of his venerable years, he had met the grim old wreck of Colonel Dabney, moving goutily, and gathering wrath anew with every touch of his painful foot to the ground; or driving by in his carriage, showing an ashen, angry, wrinkled face at the window, and frowning at him—the apothecary thought— with a peculiar fury, as if he took umbrage at his audacity in being less broken by age than a gentleman like himself. The apothecary could not help feeling as if there were some unsettled quarrel or dispute between himself and the Colonel, he could not tell what or why. The Colonel always gave him a haughty nod of half-recognition; and the people in the street, to whom he was a familiar object, would say, "The worshipful Colonel begins to find himself mortal like the rest of us. He feels his years." "He'd be glad, I warrant," said one, "to change with you, Doctor. It shows what difference a good life makes in men, to look at him and you. You are half a score of years his elder, me-thinks, and yet look what temperance can do for a man. By my credit, neighbor, seeing how brisk you have been lately, I told my wife you seemed to be growing younger. It does me good to see it. We are about of an age, I think, and I like to notice how we old men keep young and keep one another in heart. I myself—ahem—ahem—feel younger this season than for these five years past."

"It rejoices me that you feel so," quoth the apothecary, who had just been thinking that this neighbor of his had lost a great deal, both in mind and body, within a short period, and rather scorned him for it. "Indeed, I find old age less uncomfortable than I supposed. Little Pansie and I make excellent companions for one another."

And then, dragged along by Pansie's little hand, and also impelled by a certain alacrity that rose with him in the morning, and lasted till his healthy rest at night, he bade farewell to his contemporary, and hastened on; while the latter, left behind, was somewhat irritated as he looked at the vigorous movement of the apothecary's legs.

"He need not make such a show of briskness neither," muttered he to himself. "This touch of rheumatism troubles me a bit just now, but try it on a good day, and I'd walk with him for a shilling. Pshaw! I'll walk to his funeral yet."

One day, while the Doctor, with the activity that bestirred itself in him nowadays, was mixing and manufacturing certain medicaments that came in frequent demand, a carriage stopped at his door, and he recognized the voice of Colonel Dabney, talking in his customary stern tone to the woman who served him. And, a moment afterwards, the coach drove away, and he actually heard the old dignitary lumbering up stairs, and bestowing a curse upon each particular step, as if that were the method to make them soften and become easier when he should come down again. "Pray, your worship," said the Doctor from above, "let me attend you below stairs."

"No," growled the Colonel, "I'll meet you on your own ground. I can climb a stair yet, and be hanged to you."

So saying, he painfully finished the ascent, and came into the laboratory, where he let himself fall into the Doctor's easy-chair, with an anathema on the chair, the Doctor, and himself; and, staring round through the dusk, he met the wide-open, startled eyes of little Pansie, who had been reading a gilt picture-book in the corner.

"Send away that child, Dolliver," cried the Colonel, angrily. "Confound her, she makes my bones ache. I hate everything young."

"Lord, Colonel," the poor apothecary ventured to say, "there must be young people in the world as well as old ones. 'T is my mind, a man's grandchildren keep him warm round about him."

"I have none, and want none," sharply responded the Colonel; "and as for young people, let me be one of them, and they may exist, otherwise not. It is a cursed bad arrangement of the world, that there are young and old here together."

When Pansie had gone away, which she did with anything but reluctance, having a natural antipathy to this monster of a Colonel, the latter personage tapped with his crutch-handled cane on a chair that stood near, and nodded in an authoritative way to the apothecary to sit down in it. Dr. Dolliver complied submissively, and the Colonel, with dull, unkindly eyes, looked at him sternly, and with a kind of intelligence amid the aged stolidity of his aspect, that somewhat puzzled the Doctor. In this way he surveyed him all over, like a judge, when he means to hang a man, and for some reason or none, the apothecary felt his nerves shake, beneath this steadfast look.

"Aha! Doctor!" said the Colonel at last, with a doltish sneer, "you bear your years well."

"Decently well, Colonel; I thank Providence for it," answered the meek apothecary.

"I should say," quoth the Colonel, "you are younger at this moment than when we spoke together two or three years ago. I noted then that your eyebrows were a handsome snow-white, such as befits a man who has passed beyond his threescore years and ten, and five years more. Why, they are getting dark again, Mr. Apothecary."

"Nay, your worship must needs be mistaken there," said the Doctor, with a timorous chuckle. "It is many a year since I have taken a deliberate note of my wretched old visage in a glass, but I remember they were white when I looked last."

"Come, Doctor, I know a thing or two," said the Colonel, with a bitter scoff; "and what's this, you old rogue? Why, you've rubbed away a wrinkle since we met. Take off those infernal spectacles, and look me in the face. Ha! I see the devil in your eye. How dare you let it shine upon me so?"

"On my conscience, Colonel," said the apothecary, strangely struck with the coincidence of this accusation with little Pansie's complaint, "I know not what you mean. My sight is pretty well for a man of my age. We near-sighted people begin to know our best eyesight, when other people have lost theirs."

"Ah! ah! old rogue," repeated the insufferable Colonel, gnashing his ruined teeth at him, as if, for some incomprehensible reason, he wished to tear him to pieces and devour him. "I know you. You are taking the life away from me, villain! and I told you it was my inheritance. And I told you there was a Bloody Footstep, bearing its track down through my race.

"I remember nothing of it," said the Doctor, in a quake, sure that the Colonel was in one of his mad fits. "And on the word of an honest man, I never wronged you in my life, Colonel."

"We shall see," said the Colonel, whose wrinkled visage grew absolutely terrible with its hardness; and his dull eyes, without losing their dulness, seemed to look through him.

"Listen to me, sir. Some ten years ago, there came to you a man on a secret business. He had an old musty bit of parchment, on which were written some words, hardly legible, in an antique hand,—an old deed, it might have been,— some family document, and here and there the letters were faded away. But this man had spent his life over it, and he had made out the meaning, and he interpreted it to you, and left it with you, only there was one gap,—one torn or obliterated place. Well, sir,—and he bade you, with your poor little skill at the mortar, and for a certain sum,—ample repayment for such a service,—to manufacture this medicine,—this cordial. It was an affair of months. And just when you thought it finished, the man came again, and stood over your cursed beverage, and shook a powder, or dropped a lump into it, or put in some ingredient, in which was all the hidden virtue,—or, at least, it drew out all the hidden virtue of the mean and common herbs, and married them into a wondrous efficacy. This done, the man bade you do certain other things with the potation, and went away"—the Colonel hesitated a moment—"and never came back again."

"Surely, Colonel, you are correct," said the apothecary; much startled, however, at the Colonel's showing himself so well acquainted with an incident which he had supposed a secret with himself alone. Yet he had a little reluctance in owning it, although he did not exactly understand why, since the Colonel had, apparently, no rightful claim to it, at all events.

"That medicine, that receipt," continued his visitor, "is my hereditary property, and I challenge you, on your peril, to give it up."

"But what if the original owner should call upon me for it," objected Dr. Dolliver.

"I'll warrant you against that," said the Colonel; and the apothecary thought there was something ghastly in his look and tone. "Why, 't is ten year, you old fool; and do you think a man with a treasure like that in his possession would have waited so long?"

"Seven years it was ago," said the apothecary. "Septem annis passatis: so says the Latin."

"Curse your Latin," answers the Colonel. "Produce the stuff. You have been violating the first rule of your trade,—taking your own drugs,—your own, in one sense; mine by the right of three hundred years. Bring it forth, I say!"

"Pray excuse me, worthy Colonel," pleaded the apothecary; for though convinced that the old gentleman was only in one of his insane fits, when he talked of the value of this concoction, yet he really did not like to give up the cordial, which perhaps had wrought him some benefit. Besides, he had at least a claim upon it for much trouble and skill expended in its composition. This he suggested to the Colonel, who scornfully took out of his pocket a net-work purse, with more golden guineas in it than the apothecary had seen in the whole seven years, and was rude enough to fling it in his face. "Take that," thundered he, "and give up the thing, or I will have you in prison before you are an hour older. Nay," he continued, growing pale, which was his mode of showing terrible wrath; since all through life, till extreme age quenched it, his ordinary face had been a blazing-red, "I'll put you to death, you villain, as I've a right!" And thrusting his hand into his waistcoat pocket, lo! the madman took a small pistol from it, which he cocked, and presented at the poor apothecary. The old fellow, quaked and cowered in his chair, and would indeed have given his whole shopful of better concocted medicines than this, to be out of this danger. Besides, there were the guineas; the Colonel had paid him a princely sum for what was probably worth nothing.

"Hold! hold!" cried he as the Colonel, with stern eye pointed the pistol at his head. "You shall have it."

So he rose all trembling, and crept to that secret cupboard, where the precious bottle—since precious it seemed to be—was reposited. In all his life, long as it had been, the apothecary had never before been threatened by a deadly weapon; though many as deadly a thing had he seen poured into a glass, without winking. And so it seemed to take his heart and life away, and he brought the cordial forth feebly, and stood tremulously before the Colonel, ashy pale, and looking ten years older than his real age, instead of five years younger, as he had seemed just before this disastrous interview with the Colonel.

"You look as if you needed a drop of it yourself," said Colonel Dabney, with great scorn. "But not a drop shall you have. Already have you stolen too much," said he, lifting up the bottle, and marking the space to which the liquor had subsided in it in consequence of the minute doses with which the apothecary had made free. "Fool, had you taken your glass like a man, you might have been young again. Now, creep on, the few months you have left, poor, torpid knave, and die! Come—a goblet! quick!"

He clutched the bottle meanwhile voraciously, miserly, eagerly, furiously, as if it were his life that he held in his grasp; angry, impatient, as if something long sought were within his reach, and not yet secure,—with longing thirst and desire; suspicious of the world and of fate; feeling as if an iron hand were over him, and a crowd of violent robbers round about him, struggling for it. At last, unable to wait longer, just as the apothecary was tottering away in quest of a drinking-glass, the Colonel took out the stopple, and lifted the flask itself to his lips.

"For Heaven's sake, no!" cried the Doctor. "The dose is one single drop!— one drop, Colonel, one drop!"

"Not a drop to save your wretched old soul," responded the Colonel; probably thinking that the apothecary was pleading for a small share of the precious liquor. He put it to his lips, and, as if quenching a lifelong thirst, swallowed deep draughts, sucking it in with desperation, till, void of breath, he set it down upon the table. The rich, poignant perfume spread itself through the air.

The apothecary, with an instinctive carefulness that was rather ludicrous under the circumstances, caught up the stopper, which the Colonel had let fall, and forced it into the bottle to prevent any farther escape of virtue. He then fearfully watched the result of the madman's potation.

The Colonel sat a moment in his chair, panting for breath; then started to his feet with a prompt vigor that contrasted widely with the infirm and rheumatic movements that had heretofore characterized him. He struck his forehead violently with one hand, and smote his chest with the other: he stamped his foot thunderously on the ground; then he leaped up to the ceiling, and came down with an elastic bound. Then he laughed, a wild, exulting ha! ha! with a strange triumphant roar that filled the house and reechoed through it; a sound full of fierce, animal rapture,—enjoyment of sensual life mixed up with a sort of horror. After all, real as it was, it was like the sounds a man makes in a dream. And this, while the potent draught seemed still to be making its way through his system; and the frightened apothecary thought that he intended a revengeful onslaught upon himself. Finally, he uttered a loud unearthly screech, in the midst of which his voice broke, as if some unseen hand were throttling him, and, starting forward, he fought frantically, as if he would clutch the life that was being rent away,—and fell forward with a dead thump upon the floor.

"Colonel! Colonel!" cried the terrified Doctor.

The feeble old man, with difficulty, turned over the heavy frame, and saw at once, with practised eye, that he was dead. He set him up, and the corpse looked at him with angry reproach. He was so startled, that his subsequent recollections of the moment were neither distinct nor steadfast; but he fancied, though he told the strange impression to no one, that on his first glimpse of the face, with a dark flush of what looked like rage still upon it, it was a young man's face that he saw,—a face with all the passionate energy of early manhood,—the capacity for furious anger which the man had lost half a century ago, crammed to the brim with vigor till it became agony. But the next moment, if it were so (which it could not have been), the face grew ashen, withered, shrunken, more aged than in life, though still the murderous fierceness remained, and seemed to be petrified forever upon it.

After a moment's bewilderment, Dolliver ran to the window looking to the street, threw it open, and called loudly for assistance. He opened also another window, for the air to blow through, for he was almost stifled with the rich odor of the cordial which filled the room, and was now exuded from the corpse.

He heard the voice of Pansie, crying at the door, which was locked, and, turning the key, he caught her in his arms, and hastened with her below stairs, to give her into the charge of Martha, who seemed half stupefied with a sense of something awful that had occurred.

Meanwhile there was a rattling and a banging at the street portal, to which several people had been attracted both by the Doctor's outcry from the window, and by the awful screech in which the Colonel's spirit (if, indeed, he had that divine part) had just previously taken its flight.

He let them in, and, pale and shivering, ushered them up to the death-chamber, where one or two, with a more delicate sense of smelling than the rest, snuffed the atmosphere, as if sensible of an unknown fragrance, yet appeared afraid to breathe, when they saw the terrific countenance leaning back against the chair, and eying them so truculently.

I would fain quit the scene and have done with the Colonel, who, I am glad, has happened to die at so early a period of the narrative. I therefore hasten to say that a coroner's inquest was held on the spot, though everybody felt that it was merely ceremonial, and that the testimony of their good and ancient townsman, Dr. Dolliver, was amply sufficient to settle the matter. The verdict was, "Death by the visitation of God."

The apothecary gave evidence that the Colonel, without asking leave, and positively against his advice, had drunk a quantity of distilled spirits; and one or two servants, or members of the Colonel's family, testified that he had been in a very uncomfortable state of mind for some days past, so that they fancied he was insane. Therefore nobody thought of blaming Dr. Dolliver for what had happened; and, if the plain truth must be told, everybody who saw the wretch was too well content to be rid of him, to trouble themselves more than was quite necessary about the way in which the incumbrance had been removed.

The corpse was taken to the mansion in order to receive a magnificent funeral; and Dr. Dolliver was left outwardly in quiet, but much disturbed, and indeed almost overwhelmed inwardly, by what had happened.

Yet it is to be observed, that he had accounted for the death with a singular dexterity of expression, when he attributed it to a dose of distilled spirits. What kind of distilled spirits were those, Doctor? and will you venture to take any more of them?

35